OXFORD BOOKWORMS LIBRARY
Human Interest

'Who, Sir? Me, Sir?'

Stage 3 (1000 headwords)

Series Editor: Jennifer Bassett
Founder Editor: Tricia Hedge
Activities Editors: Jennifer Bassett and Christine Lindop

K. M. PEYTON

'Who, Sir? Me, Sir?'

Retold by
Diane Mowat

Illustrated by
Kate Simpson

OXFORD UNIVERSITY PRESS
2000

Oxford University Press
Great Clarendon Street, Oxford OX2 6DP

Oxford New York

Athens Auckland Bangkok Bogotá Buenos Aires Calcutta Cape Town
Chennai Dar es Salaam Delhi Florence Hong Kong Istanbul Karachi
Kuala Lumpur Madrid Melbourne Mexico City Mumbai Nairobi
Paris São Paulo Shanghai Singapore Taipei Tokyo Toronto Warsaw
and associated companies in
Berlin Ibadan

OXFORD and OXFORD ENGLISH
are trade marks of Oxford University Press

ISBN 0 19 423021 X

Original edition © K. M. Peyton 1983
First published by Oxford University Press 1983
This simplified edition © Oxford University Press 2000

Second impression 2000

First published in Oxford Bookworms 1995
This second edition published in the Oxford Bookworms Library 2000

Typeset by Wyvern Typesetting Ltd, Bristol

Printed in Spain

CONTENTS

1

How it all began

It was Sam Sylvester, a teacher at Hawkwood School, who started the trouble. Just along the road from Hawkwood there was another school called Greycoats. Parents paid a lot of money to send their children to Greycoats, and the children there were clean and tidy, wore expensive clothes, and did well in examinations.

At Hawkwood the parents did not pay any money and the children were much better at fighting than at passing examinations. They were happy about that. Passing examinations meant hard work, and who wanted to study every evening?

But Sam Sylvester was worried about the difference

between the two schools. He wanted Hawkwood to be as good as Greycoats, and he was always telling his class to work harder, to try and make a better life for themselves.

'That's the trouble with you lot,' he said to his class one day. 'You don't care about anything.'

'What do you want us to care about, sir?' asked Hoomey. He was a thin, serious child, who was too small for his age. His real name was Rossiter, but when someone spoke to him, he always said, 'Who? Me?', so everyone called him 'Hoomey'.

'I want you to have ambition,' said Sam. 'To *do* things. To *want* things.'

'What kind of things, sir?' said Nutty. Her real name was Deirdre McTavish, but everybody called her 'Nutty'. She was thirteen, had a broken nose, thick glasses, black hair and a big smile. But you had to be careful with her. She was a good fighter too.

'Anything,' said Sam. 'Anything at all. Now come on, tell me what you want in life.'

Nutty put up her hand. 'I want to be a rider in the Olympic Games before I'm twenty-one,' she said.

Nutty loved horses and riding and had her own horse, called Midnight – a present from her Uncle Bean. Midnight had been on his way to the knackers, where horses were turned into dog food. But her uncle, who worked there, had bought Midnight and given him to Nutty. She had cared for the horse, taught him to jump, and now she and Midnight often won competitions.

2

'Now come on, tell me what you want in life.'

Hoomey put up his hand too.

'Yes, Rossiter?'

'I want to go and watch Northend United play football on Saturday, sir.'

'And that's your life's ambition?' said Sam crossly. 'Well, why don't you? It isn't very difficult.'

'It's too far. And my bicycle's broken.'

'You can catch a bus, can't you?'

'It's a long walk from my house to the bus-stop, sir.'

Sam covered his face with his hands, and the class laughed.

'All right, Rossiter,' Sam said. 'I'll take you in my car. You and three friends.'

'Oh, thank you, sir!' said Hoomey.

And that was how it all started, because on the way home from the football match on Saturday, Sam stopped the car at a pub. 'I'm going in here for a drink,' he said. 'I'll bring you out some cokes if you want.'

'Yes please, sir.'

The three friends with Hoomey were Nutty, Nutty's cousin David Bean and a Sikh boy called Jazz. Hoomey hadn't invited Nutty. She just said, 'I'm your friend. I'm coming.' Nobody argued with Nutty.

The Greycoats School bus was also in the pub carpark. Inside it there were four boys, drinking cokes. 'Well, that's

The three friends with Hoomey were Nutty,
David Bean and a Sikh boy called Jazz.

4

nice,' said Sam. 'Now you can all have an intelligent conversation together.'

'We don't want to talk to *them*, sir,' Bean said.

Nutty was looking hard at the Greycoats bus. 'That boy with the fair hair and the big nose,' she said. 'He's Sebastian Smith. He's Gloria's boyfriend.' Gloria was Nutty's older sister, a gentle, beautiful girl, who always had lots of boyfriends.

Nutty pushed her face against the car window, then opened it. 'Hi, Seb!' she cried. 'It's me!'

Sebastian looked at her coldly, then opened the bus window and said, 'Get lost!'

'Have you been to the match too?' asked Nutty.

'No. We've been competing in a tetrathlon. That's a Greek word, so you won't understand it.'

'What is it? A special game for little boys?'

'It's a very difficult competition in running, swimming, shooting, and cross-country riding.'

'Where did you come? Last?'

'First out of twenty teams.' Sebastian closed the window.

'I could do all that,' Nutty said. 'Hey, Seb!'

He opened the window again.

'Do they have girls in the competition?'

'No. They're not strong enough.' He smiled unkindly, and shut the window again.

'I hate that Sebastian,' Nutty said to the others.

They waited, not very patiently, for Sam, and after a while Bean went to find him. He came back shaking his head. 'He's talking to that Greycoats teacher. Arguing about something.'

A few minutes later the two teachers came out, walked over to Sam's car and looked hard at Nutty and her friends.

'What, these four?' cried the Greycoats teacher. 'You'll never make a team out of them. One of them's a girl too. You can't use her. You'll need another boy.'

'No problem,' said Sam. '*And* we'll beat you. The two men shook hands, and Sam got into his car.

'What's all that about, sir?' asked Hoomey.

'I'll tell you on Monday,' said Sam.

On Monday morning Sam's class listened with open mouths as Sam told them his news.

'Now listen carefully, because this is very important. I want to show everybody that Hawkwood School is just as good as Greycoats School. Some people think that my plan is impossible, but I know we can do it. We're going to enter a tetrathlon team against the Greycoats School team, and I've promised that we'll beat them. The competition is next summer, so we've got almost a year to get ready. It just needs hard work. And the four people in the team—'

'I know, sir,' Nutty said excitedly. 'It's because you met the Greycoats teacher on Saturday, so it's the four of us who were in your car, isn't it? Except me, because I'm a girl. But can't I be captain, sir? Olympic teams have captains.'

'Well, all right, Deirdre,' said Sam, pleased. 'We'll need your help with the riding. So the team will be Rossiter, Bean, and Jazz – and the fourth boy will be Gary Nicholson. He's a good swimmer already.'

Hoomey suddenly sat up when he heard his name. His eyes were round with horror. 'Who, sir? Me, sir?' he said, in a frightened voice. 'But I can't swim, or ride, or shoot! I can't do any of those things!'

'You can learn,' said Sam. 'You'll have to.'

Hoomey, Jazz, Bean, and Gary looked at each other unhappily. 'Why us?' said Bean. 'It's not fair! We'll never beat Greycoats. Never in a million years!'

But everybody in the school was excited by the tetrathlon plan. Yes, Hawkwood would show that rich Greycoats crowd! Hawkwood for gold!

The other teachers thought Sam was crazy, but they agreed to help. The headteacher worried about money for all the sports lessons, but Sam said that the parents liked the idea very much. They would help to pay for everything and Mr Bean would find them some horses.

In fact, everybody was happy – except Hoomey, Jazz, Bean, and Gary.

2

The horses arrive

Soon everybody was busy. The parents put some money together and Mr Bean started to look for suitable horses at the knackers. Swimming lessons were planned, and later on there would be shooting lessons.

Hoomey couldn't believe that this awful thing was really going to happen. 'Well, when we learn to shoot,' he said miserably to Bean, 'we can shoot ourselves.'

'No, we can't,' said Bean. 'Those guns are too small. They wouldn't kill a cat.'

Nutty, as the team captain, told the boys that they were lazy and just afraid of hard work.

'You can do it if you try,' she told them.

She went with the boys to the first swimming lesson. It was not a great success. Gary could swim well, and Jazz showed promise, but the swimming teacher shook his head. 'This is going to need a lot of work,' he said to Nutty. 'Three nights a week for the next year, and I really don't have time to do it.'

'But you've got to!' cried Nutty. 'Someone must.'

Gary's older brother, Nails, was swimming at the other end of the pool. He could swim like a fish and he and Gary were at the pool every night. But nobody liked Nails. He was hard and dangerous and was always in trouble with the police. The others were afraid of him, the teachers hated him and he had no real friends. Nails and Gary had no mother. She had left home, and they lived with their father, who did not care what they did. But Gary was nicer than Nails and he laughed and smiled sometimes. Nails only laughed if someone had an accident or got hurt.

Nutty was watching Nails. He could swim really fast! Perhaps he could help them? But how could you get someone like Nails to help?

Hoomey hadn't been in the water yet, and the swimming teacher shouted, 'Get in, young Rossiter!'

As Hoomey slid into the water, he thought that his last hour had come. He felt the water close over him like death, and he opened his mouth to scream. Suddenly Nails appeared. He caught Hoomey by the chin and pulled his head up out of the water. 'You stupid fool!' Nails shouted. 'Use your

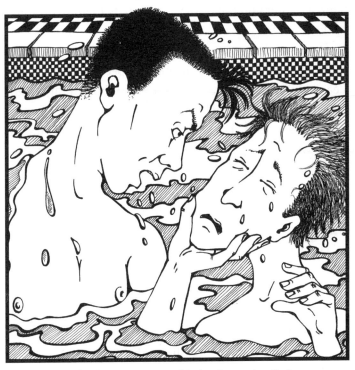

Nails caught Hoomey by the chin and pulled his head up out of the water.

9

arms!' Then he swam away. Nutty stared after him thoughtfully.

That evening Mr Bean's horses arrived. The plan was to keep them in an old, unused factory on the edge of the town. All the buildings around the factory had been destroyed and grass was growing where there were once houses. So, after tea, Nutty went down there on Midnight. When she arrived, Sam Sylvester and the boys were already there, with some of the parents.

They stood in silence as the truck with the horses in it moved slowly down the road and stopped beside them. Mr Bean got down from the driver's seat, smiling happily. 'Here we are, then,' he said. 'They don't look much, but they were good horses once. Three of them were racehorses and the other was in a circus. He'll be all right if they don't play "God Save the Queen". He lies down when they do that!' Mr Bean laughed. 'Well, let's have a look at them, then. But don't get too excited,' he added. 'Just give them three months with good food and you won't know them.'

The parents went to open the back of the truck and Hoomey stood there, trying to pretend that he did not really care. But why were his legs shaking like that? Perhaps he was really ill. Perhaps he should go to the doctor and . . .

'Mind your backs! Mind your backs!'

A very large horse was pulling Mr Bean down from the truck. It slid onto the road, looked for the nearest bit of grass and went straight towards it, pulling Mr Bean after it. Hoomey happened to be standing on that bit of grass, thinking he was safe. He saw the horse's big hungry mouth coming towards his ankles and he jumped back. Then he stood there, unable to speak, as Mr Bean pushed the horse's rope into his hand.

'He likes you. He's chosen you really, hasn't he? Here, he's yours,' Mr Bean said to Hoomey.

The horse was hungrily eating every plant and every bit of grass that it could find. It was brown, and Hoomey could see all its bones. Its legs were covered with old cuts, and there were some new ones too that were still bleeding. Its eyes were red. Hoomey stood there, holding the rope. He was too frightened to move. But the horse wanted to move

Mr Bean pushed the horse's rope into Hoomey's hand.

11

on to some new grass. It lifted a foot as big as a dinner plate and put it down near Hoomey's shoe. Hoomey jumped.

'It could break your foot like that. It's dangerous. I don't want it,' cried Hoomey, frightened.

'Well, you've got it, haven't you?' said Jazz. 'I hope mine's prettier.'

'Yours is the circus horse,' laughed Mr Bean.

Jazz watched miserably as Mr Bean brought out an extraordinary white horse covered in black spots. It wasn't as big as Hoomey's, but it was as thin. It stood there, looking very sorry for itself, and refusing to move.

'You don't see one like that every day,' said Mr Bean. 'You'll have to call him Spot,' he laughed.

Nutty sat on her beautiful Midnight, who was very different from these poor sad horses. 'It's what you make of them,' she said, trying to cheer the others up. 'Midnight looked awful when we bought him. You've got to remember that they've come straight from . . .' But she stopped there. They wouldn't want to remember that the horses had come from the knackers.

Gary and Bean were beginning to worry now. Their eyes were fixed on the truck. Mr Bean looked a bit worried too.

'This one could give us a bit of trouble,' he said. 'It's frightened. Needs a bit of love.'

There was a lot of crashing and banging from inside the truck – then a shout and a lot of bad language.

A horse shot out and hit the road. It slid round, looked around it with eyes dark with fear, and stood there, shaking.

12

A horse shot out and hit the road.

It looked a better horse than the others, but also more dangerous. Gary and Bean stepped back.

'Gary, it's the best of them all,' said Nutty, getting down from Midnight. 'Take it. It's only frightened because of the journey.'

She spoke softly to the horse. But Gary was as frightened as the horse. His face was white. Hoomey, watching, felt a bit happier. At least his horse was only large and hungry. He decided to give him the name of Bones.

But Nutty was pleased. This one looked like a good cross-country horse. 'You're lucky,' she said to Gary.

'But I want to live,' he replied.

The last horse was Bean's. It had come half-way down from the truck, and it stood there watching them with friendly, sleepy eyes. It refused to move any further, and its front feet were planted hard on the ground. It was a very big, thin, tired brown horse.

Just then Nutty saw her sister Gloria and two boys – Seb and his friend – watching from the road, and laughing at the horses.

'If you've come to spy, you can go away again!' Nutty shouted at them angrily. 'And don't laugh at the horses – they may not look much now, but they were all famous once.'

Hoomey wondered if this was true. Was his old Bones really a famous racehorse?

The parents were busy getting the factory ready and Hoomey began to realize that horses made work. Oh, well, the parents were probably going to do it all.

When everything was ready, the parents stood and watched as the horses were taken into their new home. There were a lot of old fridges in one corner of the factory, and the parents had pushed these together to make walls. Each horse now had its own little stable, filled with deep straw.

Bean's horse had been given the name Whizzo, because he moved so slowly. But he managed to move a lot faster

Each horse now had its own little stable, filled with deep straw.

when he realized there was food waiting for him in his new stable. And when the horses were comfortable and had eaten, a feeling of quiet happiness filled the old factory. Pleased, the parents left. Mr Bean started up the truck, shouted goodnight and drove away. The four boys were alone with Nutty.

'Right. That's it for tonight,' said Nutty. 'Tomorrow you'll have to give the horses their food and clean them out.'

The boys looked at her in surprise. '*Us?*'

'Yes. I'll meet you here at seven o'clock.'

'*Seven?*'

'I get up at six for Midnight, and I'm only a girl. So be here at seven. Or there'll be trouble.'

And she got back on Midnight and rode off.

3

The end of the competition?

That night Nails and Gary decided to go and look at Gary's horse. It was after midnight and it was cold. A thick, gold moon was coming up over the sea and everything was silent. Gary pushed back the big doors and moonlight filled the factory. The horses were quiet. Three of them were lying down, but Gary's mare was on her feet, walking about, and Gary and Nails stood and watched her. 'She's pretty,' Nails said after a time. 'What are you going to call her?'

'I don't know.'

'Well, you'll have to think of something.'

'Come on,' said Gary. 'It's after midnight and I've got to be back here at seven.'

'You're crazy,' said Nails.

But a few nights later, Nails went back to the factory. It wasn't comfortable at home now his mother had left. There were no meals, no warm fires to sit by, nothing. So, late one evening, he decided to go and have another look at Gary's mare.

When he closed the factory doors behind him, he was filled with a feeling of peace. He listened to the gentle sound of the horses eating. Gary's mare stopped when she heard Nails, and her ears went back.

'What's the matter, beautiful?' Nails said. 'Don't be afraid. You're all right, you know. You're not on your way to the knackers now.'

He sat down quietly beside her. Her life was a little like his, he thought. And while he sat there, the mare seemed to grow calmer. She pushed her head forward to look at him, but when he moved, she jumped back, afraid. Then, slowly, she put her face near his again, and he felt a wet tongue on his hand. Nails was pleased. 'You like me, don't you?' he said, and he could see that she did. Well, she was lucky. They were going to kill her, but now here she was – warm and comfortable. They should call her Lucky. Lucky Something. He lay back comfortably while he thought about it. The other horses moved about quietly, and it was like

Nails, unsmiling and silent, went with them to the riding school.

being in a family, by the fireside. What about Lucky Fireside . . . no, Firelight? Lucky Firelight? Lucky *Lady* Firelight. That was it! It was a good name! He wished he could ride her – well, perhaps he could. He could learn to ride, couldn't he? But the others mustn't know.

The next morning, Hoomey went up to the factory early to feed old Bones – and he found Nails asleep next to the brown mare. 'I'll kill you if you tell anyone!' Nails said. Hoomey didn't tell, but he thought it was very strange. And Nutty was very interested to find that when they went to the riding school for their first lesson, Nails, unsmiling and silent, went along with them.

The horses at the riding school looked strong and healthy, with shining coats. They were also smaller and much easier to manage than their horses at the factory. Hoomey didn't have to worry about watching out for Bones's big feet and his ever-hungry mouth. But he wanted to be able to ride Bones, and he enjoyed his first lesson very much. Nutty just stood by the wall with Nails and Mr Sylvester, and watched. She could see Hoomey was not a natural rider, and she realized how hard it was going to be. They had several months before the competition, but their own horses were old and tired, and her team was awful!

After the lesson, Nails walked with Nutty to her bus stop. 'I want to ask you something,' he said. 'Will you teach me how to ride?' He spoke almost angrily. 'I'll pay you,' he added, 'but I want it to be a secret. Don't tell the others . . . or I'll kill you!'

19

Nutty was silent with surprise, but she agreed and a week later they met for their first lesson. Nails was angry most of the time because he hated taking orders from anyone. But he learnt quickly, and Nutty agreed to continue with the lessons.

Two weeks later, one afternoon after school, the teacher from the riding school came to look at the knackers horses. The horses were taken out and the boys walked them up and down while the teacher watched.

'You must be crazy!' she cried to Sam Sylvester. 'You can't use these horses. You'll have to use mine, and, with the lessons, that'll cost you fifty pounds a week, from now until the summer!'

Nothing happened for almost a week after that, but then Sam called the team together.

'The school has decided that fifty pounds is too much,' he told them. 'The competition was a wonderful idea, of course, but the riding's too expensive. There are the swimming lessons as well, and we haven't even started the shooting yet. No, it's all too difficult. The competition's dead.'

4

The new team

Bean and Gary were pleased, Jazz did not say anything, and Hoomey was very happy – until Nutty told him that the horses would have to go back to the knackers.

Nutty was wildly angry. 'Isn't that just like adults?' she said. 'They tell you to *do* things, they get all excited, and then suddenly say it's all too difficult.'

But Hoomey was thinking about Bones. He was no longer frightened of his large, hungry horse and he knew that Bones was really a very friendly animal. It was a nice feeling when Bones pushed him gently with his nose, asking for the sugar in Hoomey's pocket. Hoomey realized, very strongly, that he did not want Bones to become dog food.

'They can't kill poor old Bones!' he cried. 'And what about Nails? What will he say about Lucky Lady Firelight? He sleeps in her stable every night now.'

'They can't kill poor old Bones!' Hoomey cried.

21

Nutty looked at Hoomey. 'Now, there's an idea,' she said softly. 'Nails . . . He could be in the team! He's going to be a good rider, and he's an excellent swimmer – he can teach the rest of us! And I'll be in the team too. Never mind that rubbish about not having girls. I can ride better than anyone at Greycoats.' She turned to Hoomey, her eyes bright with excitement. 'Will you go on with the competition, if that will save Bones?' she asked.

Hoomey thought about it. 'Yes,' he said slowly. 'Yes, I will.'

Nutty went to find Nails and explained her idea to him. You had to be careful with Nails. He could get very angry for no reason. It was hard to like him.

Nails looked at Nutty coldly. 'They won't want me in their team,' he said.

'It's not *their* team any more. It's us, our team. If we want to do the competition, they can't stop us. And we can beat Greycoats – I know we can.'

She waited hopefully, but Nails said nothing.

'Your brother Gary and Bean aren't interested,' Nutty said, 'but Jazz will go on, I think. And Hoomey. And it's the only way to save the horses.'

'OK,' Nails said at last. 'I'll do it.' He did not look at Nutty, and walked away, his hands in his pockets.

Jazz agreed to the plan as well, but said the riding was too difficult for him. Nutty began to worry, and decided to go and see what Uncle Bean thought.

'Well, I think that riding teacher was a bit hard on your

horses,' he said. 'After all, you only want to ride across country for a mile or two. You need that niece of hers – Biddy Bedwelty. She'd teach you all in a week!'

'But she's a famous competition rider! She wouldn't teach us!' replied Nutty. 'And her lessons would cost an awful lot.'

'Well, offer her Whizzo instead of money,' said Uncle Bean. 'You can ride Midnight, so you don't need a fourth horse.'

To their surprise, Biddy agreed to help them. Not for Whizzo, but because she liked doing things that seemed impossible.

'You needn't pay me if you win,' Biddy said.

'And if we lose?' asked Nutty.

'Then you have to pay me for six months' work,' Biddy replied, and she agreed to come three times a week for two hours each time.

Nutty knew that Biddy's lessons cost ten pounds an hour – but there was no other way.

Uncle Bean agreed to pay for the horses' shoes and food. 'But I want my money back if you lose, like Biddy,' he said to Nutty.

'Add it to the bill,' Nutty said crossly. 'It's only one thousand four hundred and forty pounds. Who's worrying about a few hundred more?'

Uncle Bean shouted with laughter. 'With a bill like that, I guess the four of you will work harder than you've ever done in your lives!'

And they did. They began to work at their running. They

ran to and from school, and down to the old factory where the horses were every morning and evening. They had riding lessons with Biddy three times a week, and went swimming as often as they could.

Swimming lessons with Nails were not easy. His way of teaching was very frightening. His idea was that if you put someone who can't swim into deep water, he'll have to swim to stay alive. At their first lesson Hoomey could only swim about three metres in shallow water.

'Get in,' Nails said to Hoomey.

'But it's the deep end.'

'You just get in here and swim to where you can stand up.'

Hoomey turned to run. Nails caught him, fastened his thin arms round the shaking body and jumped in with him. Nutty was watching and tried not to scream as the water closed over Hoomey.

But Hoomey came up again with Nails beside him.

'Swim!' Nails shouted in his ear. 'Or you'll die.'

Hoomey moved his arms about wildly. Nails turned on his back and slid in the water in front of Hoomey, watching him and pushing his big toe under Hoomey's chin.

'Come on, you stupid fool, or I'll hit you.'

Hoomey tried. He didn't want to die. He swam, keeping up with Nails's feet. Every time he started to go down, Nails pulled him up with his toe. Then just when Hoomey thought he really was going to die, Nails's foot pulled him up out of the water and, with a quick push, stood him up. The water

Nails caught Hoomey, fastened his arms around him,
and jumped in with him.

was half-way up his body. He looked round and saw that
he was three-quarters of the way down the pool!

'Not bad,' said Nails carelessly.

And he left Hoomey looking down in surprise at how
far he had swum, and went over to Jazz and Bean.

But the lesson with Jazz was not so successful. Nails

decided to teach Jazz how to turn. He was standing on the side of the pool and as Jazz swam up to him, Nails put his foot on the back of Jazz's head and stepped in, taking Jazz's head with him and making Jazz turn over beautifully. But Jazz did not seem to think that this was a very good idea and he hit out at Nails under the water. He caught Nails across the face with a ring he wore. Water and blood flew about wildly everywhere, and made Nutty think of films about man-eating fish. She heard the sound of wet feet running along the side of the pool as everyone came to watch. But Nutty turned away. She did not want to see. She heard shouts, bad language, and more shouts.

Then the lifeguard saw what was happening, and jumped into the water. Suddenly, two bodies flew through the air and came to rest on the side of the pool, helped there by the lifeguard's large hand.

'And don't come back for a week, Nicholson!' he shouted after Nails.

Nails turned his bloody, angry face on Nutty.

'Is that what you want, then?' he cried.

'Shut up, Nails. You frightened him. Don't get angry. You're a great teacher, but go easy on them. Get changed and I'll buy you a coke.'

She waited for the boys, bought them something to eat and calmed them down. By then it was raining heavily and Nutty still had to take Midnight out for his ride. She ran to catch her bus, tired of having to do everything for the others.

Then the lifeguard saw what was happening.

Lessons with Biddy were also hard work. It didn't matter if it was raining or snowing; they still had the lesson. Nails could make Firelight do anything for him now. They had a very special feeling for each other, and when Biddy wanted Nails to change horses, he refused.

Nutty's sister Gloria was still seeing Sebastian Smith, and Nutty was pleased about this. She wanted a spy in the Greycoats team. One evening Gloria told Seb all about the new team, while she and Seb were sitting in the back seats in the cinema. Seb sat up suddenly and looked at Gloria in surprise.

'What?' he said. 'Nutty's in the team? And that terrible Nails? He can swim like a fish! And Colin, in our team, isn't a good swimmer at all.'

One evening Gloria told Seb all about the new team.

'And Biddy Bedwelty is teaching them riding.'

'I don't like this,' Seb said. He sounded very unhappy. 'I don't like it at all. We never thought that Hawkwood would beat us! But your sister Nutty is really dangerous when she gets an idea in her head. I think our team is going to have to do some serious hard work.'

5

The secret swimming

The Hawkwood team worked hard all through the winter months. Nutty found the swimming difficult, but she kept trying and Nails helped her. He was growing more friendly now, and with his help Nutty began to get better quickly. 'If I can ride,' he said, 'you can swim!'

It was true that Nails could ride well now, but he still refused to change horses. 'It's Firelight I'm riding in the competition,' he said. 'So why change?'

The shooting was a problem. They had no guns and the lessons were very expensive. Nutty didn't know what they were going to do about it, but the competition wasn't until August, and they *were* getting better at the other things. Jazz and Hoomey had stopped taking the bus to school and ran there every day. It was Nutty herself who found the running difficult.

So winter passed and spring came. More people started

coming to the swimming pool and this meant that it was always crowded. It was all right for Seb Smith and his team. The Smiths had a pool in their garden, so the Greycoats team could swim there. Nutty saw their pool one night when she was riding near the Smiths' house. It was down at the end of the garden, and there were trees between the pool and the house. Nutty realized that they could swim there and no one could see them from the house!

When she arrived home, she told Gloria about it.

'Well,' Gloria said, 'Friday's your night. Mr and Mrs Smith go out and Seb takes me to a film. The place is empty by seven.'

So, every Friday night, Nutty's team used the Smiths' pool. The weather was cold to begin with, and the first time that Hoomey jumped into the water, he came up with a scream. 'It's like ice!' he cried, as he tried to get out. But Nails caught him and held him round the neck. 'Get swimming!' he shouted.

But the days grew warmer, and one evening Nutty was sitting beside the pool with Nails, watching Jazz and Hoomey swimming. She was feeling pleased. Jazz was a born swimmer, she decided. She stood up and went to get a sweet from the pocket of her coat, which was over by the trees. Suddenly she heard voices on the other side of the trees. She went cold with fear.

'Come and have a look at our pool,' said the voice. 'I thought Seb had gone out, but he seems to be there.'

Nutty dropped her coat and ran back to Nails.

'Mrs Smith!' she said. 'She's coming! Get them out!'

Hoomey was just finishing. Nutty flew round the pool, got down and screamed at him, 'Hoomey! Get out!'

He looked up with his mouth open, drank half the pool and went under the water. Nutty caught him by a handful of skin and pulled him over to the side. 'The Smiths are here!' she cried. '*Quick!*'

He jumped up towards her and she pulled him out. He ran as fast as his legs would carry him. But Jazz was still going up and down in the water, and did not hear Nails's cries to get out. Mrs Smith appeared with another lady at her side, smiling.

'Hello, my dears!' she said.

They ran, leaving Jazz behind. The next minute they disappeared through a hole in the hedge. Nutty was the last

*They ran, leaving Jazz behind, and disappeared
through a hole in the hedge.*

31

to go, and she saw the smiling lady look down into the pool
and heard her say, 'Why, how brown he is! Have you been
to Spain for the holidays?'

They flew down the street, but came to a stop when an
old man, who was taking his dog for its evening walk, gave
them a very strange look.

'What shall we do?' cried Nutty. 'We've left all our clothes
there!'

They stood there with water running from them, not
knowing what to do. Three older boys were coming along
the street towards them, and a group of children on bicycles
started riding round and round them.

'Let's get home,' Nails said angrily.

'We can't leave Jazz!'

Nutty stopped and looked back, and just then Jazz
appeared through the hole in the hedge. Usually, of course,
Jazz's long hair was hidden under his turban. Sikhs never
cut their hair, and although Jazz wanted to cut his, his parents
wouldn't let him. Now, Jazz's swimming hat had fallen off,
and he looked really wild with his long wet hair falling half-
way down his body and covering his face. He came flying
towards them, and cries of 'Stop! Stop!' came from the
garden. Dogs in other gardens began to bark loudly. 'Why
didn't you tell me?' said Jazz unhappily.

A bus was coming slowly along the road. By now the
boys had started to run towards them, and the children on
bicycles, still going round and round them, were shouting
and laughing.

'Quick! Let's get out of here!' Nutty cried.

She raced along the road towards the bus stop with her arm up to stop the bus. The others ran with her. The shouting behind them grew wilder, and Nutty saw the bus driver's surprised face as the bus screamed to a stop. It was a double-decker bus, and Nutty and the others got on quickly at the back and ran upstairs.

Nutty and the others got on quickly and ran upstairs.

'We haven't bought tickets!' Hoomey said in a quiet, frightened voice.

'Let's just hope that no ticket inspector gets on,' Nutty answered.

The bus was full and everybody was looking at them. Nutty slid down in her seat, but, without clothes, there was nothing to hide her. Jazz shook his hair, which fell down over his face, and he sat there looking like some strange wild animal.

But a ticket inspector did get on at the next stop. He came up to Jazz's seat. 'Tickets, please!' he said.

Jazz began to speak very quickly in Punjabi, the language his parents used at home.

Nutty looked out of the window, hoping for more time, but the inspector came to her next.

'I've lost my handbag,' Nutty said, and she got down on the floor, looking for it.

'You never had a handbag, Madam,' the inspector said, not amused.

Hoomey was also pretending to look for his ticket under his seat, and the inspector went up to Nails next. 'Tickets, please,' he shouted. Nails did not answer. The inspector tried again, but Nails still didn't move.

'He can't hear,' Nutty explained. 'He's deaf.'

The inspector stopped the bus. 'Come on,' he said. 'Get off – the four of you. This is the sea front and that's what you must be looking for.'

'But it's cold out there!'

'Then wear some clothes next time.'

There was a cold wind down by the sea, and they all lived on the other side of town. Nails's house was the nearest, so they decided to go there and get some clothes.

The run through the centre of town was something that they would never forget. The crowds shouted with laughter when they saw this strange group, dressed only in swimming things, and Jazz with his long black hair covering his face. But they finally reached the little house where Nails lived. Some minutes later, three very strange figures left, wearing borrowed clothes which did not fit and which were years out of date.

When Nutty arrived home, she had to tell her parents what had happened. They were very angry.

'Right,' said her father. 'You can just get changed. We're going round to the Smiths' and you can tell them you're sorry about all this!'

It was all right for the others, thought Nutty miserably. They were in the factory with the horses while she, the team captain, was left with all the problems.

Her father drove her up to the rich part of town to the Smiths' house. When they arrived, Nutty was sorry to see that the lights were on. The Smiths were in – and there was no escape!

Mrs Smith opened the door. 'Well?' she said icily.

'My daughter has come to say she's sorry,' Nutty's father explained.

'Yes. Well. Come in and talk to my husband.'

Nutty did not want to go in. She hated this house. Everything showed that the Smiths had lots of money, very different from Nails's poor little house. But Seb's father seemed more friendly than angry, and Nutty said that she was sorry for using their pool secretly.

'That's all right,' said Mr Smith, 'but ask first next time.'

Then, to Nutty's surprise, he offered them a drink. He

To Nutty's surprise, Mr Smith offered them a drink.

36

wanted to know why she and her friends were using the pool, and Nutty told him all about the competition.

'Do you mean you're doing all this yourselves, with no help? Do your teachers know?'

Nutty didn't know and she didn't really care.

But Mr Smith laughed. 'I think that's wonderful, Mr McTavish,' he said to Nutty's father. 'We give Sebastian too much,' he went on. 'I've had to work for what I've got, and your Deirdre's the same. She's a worker, and she can use our pool when she wants to.' Then he asked Nutty about the shooting, and when he heard that they had no money for lessons, he said, 'Well, I'll see what I can do for you. I'll have a word with a policeman friend of mine.' He laughed again. 'It'll be good for Seb and his friends to work a bit harder.'

And for a minute Nutty almost felt sorry for Seb.

6

Riding and shooting

Mr Smith's police friend, Mr Potter, called at Hawkwood and asked for Miss Deirdre McTavish, the captain of the Hawkwood tetrathlon team. And so, to his great surprise, Sam Sylvester learned that there was still a Hawkwood team. Mr Potter had brought guns and targets with him, and was ready to start the first lesson. Everybody in the school wanted

Mr Potter had brought guns and targets with him.

to try the shooting when they saw the guns. 'Get lost!' cried
Nutty. 'None of you wanted to do the other things, so get
lost before I shoot you.'

The first lesson went well and Mr Potter agreed to come
down two or three times a week to teach them. They fixed
two nights when they weren't swimming, and that left two
nights for riding lessons, and Sunday off. Running was all
the time, and so was taking out the horses. After all this
hard work, Nutty was now much thinner, and Hoomey's
thin arms and legs were really strong. They all looked strong
and healthy, and Jazz most of all. But, although Jazz was

so good at running and swimming, he was still worried about his riding.

'We're all better at some things than others,' Nutty said to him. In fact, she thought that she was probably the worst of all of them at most things. True, she was good at riding, but that was only a quarter of the competition.

The competition would be at Swallow Hall, a big country house with its own lake and swimming pool. First there was the shooting, then the four-minute swim, the two-mile run, and the riding. In each part, only the best three scores in the team were counted. But Nutty suddenly realized that they had never tried all four parts of the competition on the same day.

They continued to work hard, and in the summer Uncle Bean found some farms where they could try some real cross-country riding. Hoomey's horse Bones loved it. He seemed to remember his past as a racehorse, and went over the jumps like an express train, nearly frightening Hoomey to death.

'You were wonderful, Hoomey,' the others told him afterwards. Hoomey's face went bright red, and he forgot that he was afraid.

Poor Jazz had problems. When Spot came to a jump, he stopped – but Jazz went on, over his head. Then Nutty remembered something. 'Spot was in a circus. Perhaps he'll do it to music.'

So they brought some music and played it, and Spot stood up on his back legs and Jazz fell off again! But, in the end, Spot jumped better to music.

Nails had no problems with Firelight. She did anything that he wanted, and when he was in the factory with her on a warm summer evening, he was really happy. He liked being with her and he was now a much nicer person. But he could not understand why he felt this way about an animal.

Firelight usually lay down and slept next to Nails, but one night she did not do this. Instead, she moved around her box all the time. Nails began to think that she was ill. He was very worried and thought of going to ask Nutty what to do about it, but then Firelight grew quieter and Nails fell asleep.

He woke suddenly. Something was wrong. Firelight was ill again. 'Oh, please don't die!' he cried silently. Then, suddenly Nails understood what was happening. Firelight was having a baby! When Nails saw the foal's little face appear, he laughed and cried at the same time. 'You lovely baby!' he said softly. This was the most exciting thing that had ever happened to him. He had to go and tell Nutty.

Nutty's father was a little surprised to see Nails standing outside his door with a great big smile on his face at a quarter to five in the morning! A sleepy Nutty appeared and Nails told her his wonderful news. To his surprise, Nutty was not as happy about the foal as he was. She knew that Nails could not ride Firelight in the competition now.

And when Nails learnt that Firelight and her foal would have to leave the factory because they needed grass, he too was unhappy. Then Uncle Bean remembered that he had

'You lovely baby!' Nails said softly.

the use of a field not far away. Firelight and her foal could go there. Nails discovered that there was a shed there too, where he could sleep, and he felt better about it. But he had lost interest in the competition, and didn't care that he had no horse to ride.

'But you have to care,' Biddy told him, almost angrily. 'It isn't just for you. You're part of a team. Everyone's worked really hard, so you have to ride for them.'

41

Biddy, in her own way, was as hard a person as Nails. The next night she came on her motor-bike to fetch him, took him to her place and began to teach him to ride Switchback, one of her horses. It was a young horse, big, fast – and very frightening. But nobody argued with Biddy, so Nails hid his fear and rode Switchback over the jumps. It felt like flying, and Nails began to realize that he had never enjoyed anything in his life as much as this. He rode every evening and spent all his free time with Firelight and her foal, Bonfire.

Biddy came on her motor-bike to fetch Nails.

There were now only three weeks to the competition. Gloria told Nutty that Seb and his team had started to work hard too.

'They're really worried,' Gloria went on. 'They'd hate to lose to the Hawkwood team, and they're going to cheat if they think you're winning. Seb told me.'

Nutty was very angry. 'That's terrible!' she said.

'Well, if they cheat, why don't you cheat too?'

'I don't know how,' said Nutty. 'But you find out their plans. I'll kill you if you don't tell me what's going on!'

7

The competition day arrives

At last the big day came. Nutty, Hoomey, and Jazz met early at the factory and began to get the horses ready. Nails was late. Perhaps he was still asleep in his field with Firelight, Nutty thought crossly.

Jazz's father was driving them to Swallow Hall, Mr Potter was meeting them there with the guns, and Uncle Bean and Biddy would arrive at lunchtime with the horses. When they were ready to go, Nails had still not arrived. Nutty began to feel sick with worry. In the end, they left without him.

'What'll we do if Nails doesn't come?' Hoomey asked.

'We'll just have to be twice as good. Right?' Nutty said bravely. 'We can do it.'

Hoomey and Jazz were silent. They all knew that Nails was their best swimmer and their best runner. Without him, they would probably fail.

Jazz had never been anywhere as grand as Swallow Hall before, and he felt that everyone was looking at his dark skin and his turban. But Nutty didn't seem to care how grand it was, although she found she was the only girl in the competition.

'It's for boys, I told you,' said Seb. He appeared out of the crowd, looking very cool. 'They don't usually let girls compete. And you haven't got a chance!'

'I know what I'm doing. Just go away, Seb dear,' Nutty replied. She turned to the others. 'Let's walk round the cross-country course,' she said. She knew she wouldn't be strong enough to do it after the swim.

Hoomey walked round smiling at all the jumps like old friends. 'Are you all right, Hoomey?' Nutty asked him, worried. But Hoomey just went on smiling.

Jazz looked miserable. 'I hate the riding,' he said.

'Spot can do it,' replied Nutty, 'if you *make* him. And you must. You and Nails are our best scorers in the other things.'

God, where was Nails?

He still wasn't there when they got back for the shooting. 'He can shoot later,' the official said.

Seb and the others were shooting and their score was not bad. Then it was Hawkwood's turn.

Nutty didn't do well at first, but then she pretended it

was Seb's face on the target. She hit his nose, his ears and his mouth, and got a much better score. Jazz did well too, but Hoomey's score was the worst. He hit Jazz's target twice!

'You know I'm no good, Nutty,' he said.

'Come on,' said Nutty. 'The swimming!' There was nothing you could do with Hoomey, except kill him!

They got changed ready for the swimming and came back to watch Seb's team. Then Hoomey realized that he'd left his goggles in the changing-room and went to get them. When he came back, Colin, one of the Greycoats team, was swimming. He was very good indeed, and Nutty stared. 'Seb said that Colin was their worst swimmer.'

'But that can't be Colin,' said Hoomey. 'I've just seen Colin in the changing-room.'

So that was why Colin was swimming so well! Everyone looked the same in goggles, and it wasn't Colin at all. They'd cheated! None of the officials noticed anything, and when

Everyone looked the same in goggles.

45

they had finished the swimming, the Greycoats team all disappeared fast. Nutty was wild with anger.

Then it was Hawkwood's turn to swim. Four minutes of hard swimming felt like a long, slow death to Nutty, but she kept going, up and down, up and down, and when it was over, they had to pull her out of the water. When at last she could see again, Jazz was swimming beautifully – but there was still no Nails.

Nutty went to get dressed and when she came out to meet the others, she looked over towards the swimming pool. And at that moment she saw a boy run in, and start talking to the swimming officials. Nutty stared. Then she shouted to the others, 'Look! There he is! Now we've got a chance of winning!'

Nails had come at last!

8

Winners and losers

Nails had already done his shooting, and now he swam wonderfully, moving fast and easily up and down the pool. It was a ten-metre pool, and Nails did thirty-four lengths in four minutes. Nutty wanted to laugh out loud with happiness.

'Not bad,' she said, when Nails had finished. 'But where have you been all this time?'

Nails looked angry. 'I was sleeping in the shed in Firelight's field last night, and the police came and got me. They asked me where I lived and I wouldn't tell them, so they locked me up in the police station all night. I had to argue my way out this morning. Biddy came to fetch me, because I told the police she was my mother. Biddy was a bit angry about that.'

Nutty wondered what would happen to Nails after today. Sleeping out in fields, no real home to go to, nothing to look forward to. But there was no time to worry about that now. There was still the running and the riding to do.

Greycoats went first in the running, and Nutty watched them angrily. 'We're well behind after that cheating,' she said. 'And just look at them now!'

Greycoats were running well. 'We've just got to keep going,' Nutty said.

And they did. But it nearly killed Nutty. Hoomey, running in front of her, grew smaller and smaller, and Nutty realized that she was probably the worst of them all. But she finished, fell to the ground and lay there with her eyes closed. When she opened them again, Biddy was there. At last! Nutty was free! Biddy would tell them all what to do now.

'You've all got to ride like crazy if you're going to beat those Greycoat boys,' Biddy said.

By now the parents had all arrived and were enjoying their day out. Uncle Bean had brought the horses, and Hoomey was looking at Bones with dreamy eyes. He was in another world again. Nails and Jazz looked worried.

Switchback, Nails's horse, looked very big and strong and would not be easy for him to ride.

When Nutty went to look at the scores, she saw that her team had fallen well behind Greycoats now. They all needed clear rounds in the riding to have any chance of winning at all. Hoomey rode past on Bones, and Nutty suddenly realized that Bones was no longer the thin, miserable horse who had come to them. His eyes shone and he looked more like a three-year-old, ready to race and to win. Little Hoomey would never be able to stop him, Nutty thought worriedly.

Greycoats began their riding, and Nutty was very pleased indeed when Seb fell into the first ditch. The rest of the Greycoats team looked worried and Nutty smiled happily. Then she saw Gloria and rode up to her. 'They cheated, didn't they?' Nutty said angrily, and Gloria looked uncomfortable.

Seb fell into the first ditch.

All four Greycoats riders did badly. 'You've really got to go well,' Nutty told her team. 'We could beat them!' But when they heard this, the others looked more worried than ever.

The Greycoats team were now having some kind of discussion, and Gloria was with them. But it was time for Nutty to go. She was riding first, then Hoomey and then Nails and Jazz. Nutty was afraid that Jazz would not get round. Spot could do it with a strong rider, but Jazz wasn't strong enough, and Nutty was worried.

The starter looked at his watch. 'Go!' he called, and Nutty had a wonderful feeling of excitement. This was what she was good at, and Midnight flew over the ground. The course seemed easy to Nutty as they went over the jumps with no trouble at all, across the next field, over the big ditch and up into the woods. Away below her on the left, she could see the main road with the cars shining in the sun. But her way was to the right and down the hill. There she had to stop, get off her horse and open a gate, while an official timed her. The official was the mother of one of the Greycoats team and her car was parked near the gate. But Nutty did well, and Midnight was off again, over the jumps and through the finish, fast and clear.

Hoomey was waiting to go, with his eyes shining as he looked at his wonderful Bones. 'Good luck!' Nutty called – and Hoomey was away. Bones went off like an express train, and there was no way he was going to stop before he heard the crowd shouting for him at the finish.

49

Just then Gloria hurried up to Nutty. 'They're going to cheat again,' she said. 'They've got a recording of "God Save the Queen". They've hidden it in the official's car, and when Spot has to stop at the gate, they're going to play it, and . . .'

'Spot will lie down,' Nutty finished. 'Don't worry,' she said to Jazz. 'You're riding last, so if Hoomey and Nails go clear, then we're all right.'

'Where is Hoomey?' Nails said, worried. 'He should be out of the woods by now. He was going very fast.'

Nutty looked towards the top of the hill. There was no Hoomey! But there was something happening – people were running about wildly and one of the officials had his red flag up – red for blood, which meant they needed an ambulance. But there were a lot of other flags too, and then cars starting up, one coming down the hill and others going up to meet it. People were shouting and looking serious.

Hoomey was in trouble, Nutty realized, and she knew that both Nails and Jazz had to get clear rounds now. But she could also see, from the look of fear on Jazz's face, that he couldn't do it.

But she knew *she could*. 'Colin cheated,' she said, 'and so will we! *I'll* ride Spot!'

The others stared at her with open mouths. 'But you're the wrong colour!' said Nails.

'Gloria's got something that she uses to make her look brown. I'll put that on my face and I'll wear Jazz's turban. Our riding clothes are all the same, and if I keep moving

One of the officials had his red flag up.

fast, no one will ever know!'

Nails went off to start his riding, and the others hurried into the back of Uncle Bean's truck. A few minutes later Nutty had become Jazz.

'I hope I don't really look like that!' said Jazz.

'You hide here until I get back,' said Nutty. 'And let's hope that Nails does a clear round!'

Nutty ran out and got onto Spot. She looked up the hill and saw Nails going well on Switchback, but there was still no Hoomey. He must be still alive, but where was he?

Then the starter called 'Go!', and Nutty was away. Spot, surprised, was galloping before he had time to think. Nutty hurried him on, and he found it easier to jump than to refuse.

They reached the wood safely, and from the top of the hill Nutty saw Nails going fast towards the finish. They could still win.

As Nutty came out of the wood, she saw the ambulances and cars and a crowd of people looking down the hill. She had no time to see what was happening, and turned Spot towards the next jump. Then Bones and Hoomey suddenly appeared, coming *up* the hill from the main road, and galloping very fast towards the jump in front of her. Bones flew over the jump, clearing it by about two metres, and Hoomey went up in the air and came down again, still on Bones's back. Now they were racing towards the gate, and Nutty, not far behind, could see that Bones wasn't going to stop until he won the race.

The official was standing near the gate, but when she saw Bones and Hoomey racing towards her, she ran back to her car. Her son, who was sitting in the car, ready to play 'God Save the Queen' for Spot, was frightened to death. He forgot how important it was to start the music, and hid under the seat! Nutty got off Spot, went through the gate, and was away before the official and her son had climbed out of their car. Hoomey had already disappeared.

Nutty rode on, a wild hope growing inside her. But she had forgotten that Jazz's parents were there with Biddy and the other parents. They would know that she wasn't Jazz! But she couldn't stop to explain, and rode on past them. She could feel Biddy's glassy stare and saw the mouths of the others fall open, but she kept going and finished with

Bones wasn't going to stop until he won the race.

a clear round. She rode straight to the truck where the others were.

Inside the truck, Nutty heard that Nails had had a clear round too. 'We've done it!' she shouted. 'We've beaten them!'

Jazz, putting on his turban again, was laughing. 'Have you heard? Hoomey rode two miles down the main road!'

'Not two miles!' said Hoomey.

'And because it was a main road, he had to go down to the roundabout before he could come back.'

'What! Hoomey, you didn't!'

'Bones jumped over on to the road. I couldn't stop him.' Hoomey was white and shining when he spoke.

'And you went round the roundabout?'

Hoomey looked a bit uncomfortable. 'I thought it was the right thing to do, but the traffic was a bit cross. But Nutty, Bones was wonderful!'

By now, Nutty had cleaned her face and she felt wonderful too. 'We won!' she cried. 'We won!'

'We cheated,' Nails said.

'So did they. It's fair, if you all cheat.'

Nutty looked at Nails. He was smiling, actually *smiling*. It had been a great day for all of them, Nutty decided. Then she saw everybody walking towards them. There were all the parents, Biddy, the Greycoats teacher and Sam Sylvester – and Seb and his team.

'You cheated!' Seb called out to Nutty.

'Oh yes?' Nutty said. 'Who cheated?'

'You rode twice.'

'And you went round the roundabout?'

'And Colin didn't swim.'

'You can't be sure about that. Nobody will believe you.'

'Well, you can't be sure that I rode twice.'

'Everybody could see it was you. It's the way you ride. We'll tell the competition officials.'

'And we'll tell them about Colin not swimming. And we'll get someone to look at "God Save the Queen" in Antony's mum's car by the gate.'

'Have you all gone crazy?' Biddy asked sweetly.

The adults were all staring at the two teams, some amused, some not understanding. The Greycoats teacher looked cross. 'If there's been some cheating, then there are no real winners or losers,' he said, 'and you'll all have to do the competition again next year.'

55

'That's just what I think,' said Biddy.

The eight competitors looked at each other and fell silent in horror. Nutty couldn't believe it. The pain of all that running and swimming when you were half-dead . . .

But the adults loved the idea. They had had a nice day out, and thought that tetrathlon sports were very good for young people. They all began to make plans. Sam Sylvester said that the school would help next time, and Biddy told Nutty to forget about the money for the riding lessons.

The talking and laughing went on for some time as the adults discussed the day. 'And did you see old Bones,' said Uncle Bean, 'galloping down the main road? Even the police car couldn't catch him! What a horse!'

And that was how it all ended. No winners, no losers.

'You'll all have to do the competition again next year.'

Except that Jazz was invited by the Greycoats teacher to join a competition swimming team. And Jazz was very pleased about that because he really liked swimming. And Biddy offered Nails a job riding her horses, a room to sleep in, and a home for Firelight and her foal. Nails didn't say much but he smiled. And Nutty knew that she had been a good captain. Perhaps one day she would be the captain of an Olympic riding team. And Hoomey – well, Hoomey knew what he wanted in life now. Who said he had no ambition? The dreamy look was back in his eyes. He could be a famous rider, flying over the jumps on his horse like a bird of freedom . . .

Perhaps tomorrow everything would seem different. But today . . . today was all right.

GLOSSARY

ambition   a strong wish about what you want to do in your life

believe   to think that something is true

circus   people and animals who travel around from place to place to amuse people

compete   to try to win, or to do better than other people

competition   a game, or sport, that people try to win

course   the ground where a race is run

double-decker bus   a tall bus with seats upstairs and downstairs

examination   a test of what someone knows or can do

fool   someone who is stupid

gallop   to ride or move (for a horse) very fast

horror   a strong feeling of fear or worry

knackers   a place where old horses are killed and made into dog food

mare   a female horse

race   a competition to see who can run, ride, drive, etc. the fastest

recording   music, songs, or sounds on a record or a cassette

score   the number of points or wins that you get in a competition or sport

shed   a small wooden building on a farm, in a garden, etc.

slide (past tense **slid**)   to move quickly and easily, like moving on ice

stare   to look hard at something for a long time

target   a thing that you try to hit when shooting a gun

team   a group of people who play a sport or a game together against another group

'Who, Sir? Me, Sir?'

ACTIVITIES

Before Reading

1 Read the back cover of the book, and the story introduction on the first page. What do you know now about this story? Choose (T) true or (F) false for each sentence.

1 Sam Sylvester wants his class at Hawkwood School to be rich. T/F

2 Students at Greycoats School are from rich families. T/F

3 The competition is in four different sports. T/F

4 Sam's team are really pleased about the competition. T/F

5 They are all good swimmers already. T/F

6 They haven't done a lot of running before. T/F

7 They think their teacher has gone mad. T/F

8 They are lazy about preparing for the competition. T/F

2 Can you guess what happens on the day of the competition? Choose some of these possibilities.

1 The Hawkwood team win the competition.

2 The Greycoats team win, and Hawkwood come second.

3 Hawkwood come last out of all the teams.

4 Hawkwood don't win, but they beat Greycoats.

5 There is quite a lot of cheating in the competition.

6 The competition is stopped because of an accident.

7 Someone falls off in the cross-country riding.

8 There are no winners and no losers.

While Reading

Read Chapters 1 to 3. Choose the best question-words for these questions, and then answer them.

What / Who / Why

1 . . . were Nutty's and Hoomey's ambitions?
2 . . . did Nutty talk to in the pub carpark?
3 . . . was the plan that Sam told his class about on Monday?
4 . . . was Hoomey so frightened by this plan?
5 . . . could swim like a fish?
6 . . . kind of horses were they?
7 . . . was going to take care of the horses?
8 . . . things did Nails do that surprised Hoomey, and Nutty?
9 . . . did Sam tell the team that the competition was dead?

Before you read Chapter 4 (*The new team*), can you guess what will happen next? Choose answers to these questions.

1 Who will be in the new team? Choose four names.
  Nutty / Gloria / Bean / Nails / Gary / Jazz / Hoomey
2 Who will be the captain of the new team? Choose a name.
  Nutty / Gloria / Bean / Nails / Gary / Jazz / Hoomey
3 Who will offer to help the new team? Choose some names.
  *the riding school teacher / a famous rider / Uncle Bean /
  all the parents / Sam Sylvester / the Greycoats teacher /
  the Hawkwood headteacher / Sebastian Smith's father*

Read Chapters 4 and 5. Who said these words, and to whom?
Who or what were they talking about?

1 'They can't kill poor old Bones!'
2 'They won't want me in their team.'
3 'She'd teach you all in a week!'
4 'Then you have to pay me for six months' work.'
5 'But it's the deep end.'
6 'And don't come back for a week!'
7 'You're a great teacher, but go easy on them.'
8 'I don't like this. I don't like it at all.'
9 'Friday's your night . . . The place is empty by seven.'
10 'Mrs Smith! She's coming! Get them out!'
11 'Why didn't you tell me?'
12 'You never had a handbag, Madam.'
13 'My daughter has come to say she's sorry.'
14 'Do you mean you're doing all this yourselves, with no
   help?'

Before you read Chapter 6, how do you think the team are
doing? Complete the passage with these words.

rider / riding / running / shooting / swimmer / swimming

Because of Mr Smith, they will all have _____ lessons. Nutty
is the best _____, but will still find the _____ and the _____
difficult. Nails is now very good at _____ and is the best
_____ of them all. Jazz is good at _____ and at _____, but is
still afraid of _____. Hoomey isn't terribly good at anything,
but he enjoys _____ because he likes Bones.

Read Chapters 6 and 7. Are these sentences true (T) or false (F)? Rewrite the false ones with the right information.

1 In each part of the competition all four scores in the team were counted.

2 All of the team were better at some things than others.

3 When Firelight's foal was born, Nails was very surprised.

4 Nails couldn't ride Firelight so he lost interest in horses.

5 When Nails rode Biddy's horse Switchback over the jumps, he realized that he didn't like riding at all.

6 On the day of the competition Nails was late.

7 In the shooting Nutty and Jazz did badly, but Hoomey got a very high score.

8 The Greycoats team cheated when one of them swam instead of Colin.

Before you read the last chapter, what do you think happens in the rest of the competition? Choose Y (yes) or N (no) for each of these ideas.

1 Bones runs away and Hoomey can't stop him. Y/N

2 Somebody plays a recording of 'God Save the Queen' and Spot lies down in the middle of the course. Y/N

3 Nutty jumps a clear round on Midnight. Y/N

4 Nails falls off Switchback at the first fence. Y/N

5 The Greycoats team do well in the riding. Y/N

6 The Hawkwood team cheat in the riding. Y/N

7 Nobody finds out about the cheating and the Hawkwood team win. Y/N

After Reading

1 **What did Sam say to the Greycoats teacher (Peter) in the pub that day? Put their conversation in the right order, and write in the speakers' names. Peter speaks first (number 3).**

1 _____ 'Thank you, Sam. Of course, we do take sport very seriously at Greycoats. Not like Hawkwood.'

2 _____ 'Of course they can. A Hawkwood team could beat your boys in a tetrathlon any day. No problem.'

3 _____ 'Hullo, Sam. What have you been doing today?'

4 _____ 'Well done. You must be very pleased.'

5 _____ 'Oh, come on, Sam! They couldn't do a tetrathlon! They can't shoot, run, swim, and ride – can they?'

6 _____ 'They weren't playing. I took them to watch the Northend United match. And what about you?'

7 _____ 'In the carpark? Right, let's go and look at them!'

8 _____ 'I took some Hawkwood children to the football.'

9 _____ 'Our boys have been competing in a tetrathlon today. They came first, too.'

10 _____ 'Listen. I'll enter a team next year. I've got four children out there in my car – they could do it.'

11 _____ 'Football? Who was your team playing against?'

12 _____ 'What do you mean, not like Hawkwood? Our children are very good at all kinds of sport!'

13 _____ 'Beat our Greycoats team? Not a chance, Sam!'

2 Here is a Hawkwood school report. How many marks out of 10 would *you* give to each person in the team? Put a number in each box (1/10 is the worst, 10/10 is the best). Then use the phrases below to write a short report about each person.

	Shooting	Running	Swimming	Riding
Nutty				
Jazz				
Nails				
Hoomey				

- tries hard
- could do better
- has done well at
- is excellent at
- has worked hard at
- doesn't find . . . easy
- needs to work harder at

3 Here is Sam, telling the headteacher at Hawkwood what happened at the competition. Use these linking words to complete what he says. (You won't need all of them.)

although / and / because / before / but / so / that / what / when / where / which / who / why

'_____ our team didn't win the competition, we all had a great day out _____ everybody enjoyed themselves. The most exciting part of the day was _____ young Rossiter galloped down the main road _____ he couldn't stop his horse! I'm not really sure _____ happened at the end. Both teams said _____ the other team had cheated, _____ it's not clear _____ did what. We can't have cheating, of course, _____ we told them they would have to do the competition again next year.'

4 There are 24 words (4 letters or longer) from the story in this word search. The words go from left to right, and from top to bottom. Find them and draw lines through them.

I	G	A	L	L	O	P	T	C	R	A	Z	Y	S
A	F	C	O	M	P	E	T	I	T	I	O	N	A
M	F	A	C	T	O	R	Y	S	H	E	D	S	S
B	O	P	I	A	R	L	I	H	E	S	S	C	T
I	A	T	U	R	B	A	N	O	D	T	W	O	A
T	L	A	F	G	E	Z	Y	O	G	R	I	R	B
I	J	I	O	E	A	Y	U	T	E	A	M	E	L
O	U	N	A	T	T	R	I	D	E	W	L	L	E
N	M	C	H	R	O	U	N	D	A	B	O	U	T
E	P	O	O	L	A	T	G	O	G	G	L	E	S

1 Which two words are things you wear, and how did these things help the teams to cheat?

2 Which three words are kinds of building, and what unusual things happened in two of them?

5 Look at the word search again and write down all the letters that don't have a line through them. Begin with the first line and go across each line to the end. You should have 20 letters, which will make a sentence of 6 words.

1 What is the sentence, and who said it, to whom?

2 What was the person talking about?

3 Do you agree with the idea in the sentence? Explain why, or why not.

6 Here are some of the thoughts of the Hawkwood team. Fill in the gaps with one suitable word, and then say who is thinking, and what is happening in the story at this moment.

1 'It's really lucky I was sleeping in the _____. It was the most _____ thing I've ever seen, watching that lovely little _____ appear. I can't wait to tell Nutty the news . . .'

2 'Whew, think I'll stop for a rest. But where are the others? Why am I the only one in the _____? Who's that? Oh no! I'll have to run for the _____ – no time to get my clothes.'

3 'Boys! They're so _____! Their faces when I told them to be here at seven in the morning! It's just as well I'm the team's _____ – somebody's got to make them work . . .'

4 'It's no good, I can't stop him. We'll have to go down to the _____, turn round and come back up the other side of the road. Oh dear, there's a police car . . .'

7 What did you think about this story? Fill in some names, and complete these sentences in your own words.

1 I *liked / didn't like* _____ because _____.
2 I thought _____ was *right / wrong* to _____.
3 I felt sorry for _____ *when / because* _____.
4 I thought it was *funny /sad* when _____.
5 The part of the story I liked *most / least* was _____.
6 I *liked / didn't like* the ending because _____.

ABOUT THE AUTHOR

K. M. Peyton was born Kathleen Wendy Herald in Birmingham in 1929. As a child, she very much wanted to own a horse, but this was not possible, so at the age of nine she began to write about horses instead. She wrote her first children's novel, *Sabre, the Horse from the Sea*, when she was fifteen and it was published two years later. Two more novels followed while she was studying art at Manchester Art School. She married a fellow student, Michael Peyton, and for a time the two of them wrote adventure stories together, under the pen name of K. M. Peyton (the M is for Michael).

The first book that Mrs Peyton wrote on her own was *Windfall* (1962), a story about fishing under sail, and since then she has written over fifty books. Her three famous *Flambards* stories became a successful television series in 1978, and the second volume, *The Edge of the Cloud*, won the 1969 Carnegie Medal, an important yearly prize for children's books. Another very successful series of books was about a wild, but clever schoolboy called Pennington. Many more stories have followed, including 'Who, Sir? Me, Sir?' (1983), and *Darkling* (1989), a teenage love story set in the racing world.

All her life K. M. Peyton has had a deep love for horses, while her husband's interest has been in boats. Although she says she writes books 'to get away from boats and horses', many of her stories do in fact involve these subjects. And she has never dropped the M for Michael from her pen name because she says her husband was always making her go off on crazy adventures, which gave her wonderful material for her writing.

ABOUT BOOKWORMS

OXFORD BOOKWORMS LIBRARY
Classics • True Stories • Fantasy & Horror • Human Interest
Crime & Mystery • Thriller & Adventure

The OXFORD BOOKWORMS LIBRARY offers a wide range of original and adapted stories, both classic and modern, which take learners from elementary to advanced level through six carefully graded language stages:

Stage 1 (400 headwords)	**Stage 4** (1400 headwords)
Stage 2 (700 headwords)	**Stage 5** (1800 headwords)
Stage 3 (1000 headwords)	**Stage 6** (2500 headwords)

More than fifty titles are also available on cassette, and there are many titles at Stages 1 to 4 which are specially recommended for younger learners. In addition to the introductions and activities in each Bookworm, resource material includes photocopiable test worksheets and Teacher's Handbooks, which contain advice on running a class library and using cassettes, and the answers for the activities in the books.

———————————

Several other series are linked to the OXFORD BOOKWORMS LIBRARY. They range from highly illustrated readers for young learners, to playscripts, non-fiction readers, and unsimplified texts for advanced learners.

Oxford Bookworms Starters	*Oxford Bookworms Factfiles*
Oxford Bookworms Playscripts	*Oxford Bookworms Collection*

Details of these series and a full list of all titles in the OXFORD BOOKWORMS LIBRARY can be found in the *Oxford English* catalogues. A selection of titles from the OXFORD BOOKWORMS LIBRARY can be found on the next pages.

BOOKWORMS • THRILLER & ADVENTURE • STAGE 3

The Crown of Violet

GEOFFREY TREASE

Retold by John Escott

High up on a stone seat in the great open-air theatre of Athens, Alexis, son of Leon, watches the Festival of Plays – and dreams of seeing his own play on that famous stage.

So, as the summer passes, Alexis writes his play for the next year's Festival. But then, with his friend Corinna, he learns that Athens has enemies – enemies who do not like Athenian democracy, and who are planning a revolution to end it all . . .

BOOKWORMS • THRILLER & ADVENTURE • STAGE 3

On the Edge

GILLIAN CROSS

Retold by Clare West

When Tug wakes up, he is not in his own bedroom at home. The door is locked and there are bars across the window. Loud music hammers through the house and through his head. Then a woman comes in and says that she is his mother, but Tug knows that she is *not* his mother . . .

Outside, Jinny stares through the trees at the lonely house on the hill. She hears strange noises, but she turns away. After all, it's none of her business . . .

The Star Zoo

HARRY GILBERT

In our world today a hummingbird is a small, brilliantly coloured bird that lives in the tall trees of tropical forests.

In the far distant future, Hummingbird (Hummy for short) is a girl of sixteen who lives somewhere in the Galaxy, on a planet called Just Like Home. She has the name 'Hummingbird' in big letters on all her clothes, but she has never seen a real hummingbird. She has never seen any living animal or bird at all. The Book of Remembering says that there were once many animals on a planet called Earth, but that was before the Burning, a long, long time ago . . .

The Wind in the Willows

KENNETH GRAHAME

Retold by Jennifer Bassett

Down by the river bank, where the wind whispers through the willow trees, is a very pleasant place to have a lunch party with a few friends. But life is not always so peaceful for the Mole and the Water Rat. There is the time, for example, when Toad gets interested in motor-cars – goes mad about them in fact . . .

The story of the adventures of Mole, Rat, Badger, and Toad has been loved by young and old for almost a hundred years.

Tooth and Claw

SAKI

Retold by Rosemary Border

Conradin is ten years old. He lives alone with his aunt. He has two big secrets. The first is that he hates his aunt. The second is that he keeps a small wild animal in the garden shed. The animal has sharp white teeth, and it loves fresh blood. Every night, Conradin prays to this animal and asks it to do one thing for him, just one thing.

This collection of short stories is clever, funny, and shows us 'Nature, red in tooth and claw'. In other words, it is Saki at his very best.

Three Men in a Boat

JEROME K. JEROME

Retold by Diane Mowat

'I like work. I find it interesting . . . I can sit and look at it for hours.'

With ideas like this, perhaps it is not a good idea to spend a holiday taking a boat trip up the River Thames. But this is what the three friends – and Montmorency the dog – decide to do. It is the sort of holiday that is fun to remember afterwards, but not so much fun to wake up to early on a cold, wet morning.

This famous book has made people laugh all over the world for a hundred years . . . and they are still laughing.